HELLO, MY NAME IS
OLIVER

PAYMANEH RITCHIE

Hello, My Name Is Oliver
Copyright © 2016 by Paymaneh Ritchie

Tellwell Talent
www.tellwell.ca

ISBN
978-1-77302-250-5 (Hardcover)
978-1-77302-251-2 (Paperback)

CONTENTS

For Ea

THE BEGINNING

My name is Oliver. I was born on December 17th 2011, which according to the wise Chinese astrologers is The Year of the Rabbit. This may partially explain why I like to chase and cuddle those little bunnies!! I am what you may describe as a very handsome dog. My Beagle ears melt any heart and my shiny, black, soft Springer Spaniel fur is the envy of all dogs and humans alike. That's right; I am a cross!! (An auspicious sign, I hope!). Sometimes I think my good looks as a puppy were a curse. Not only did I sweep the floors with my generously long ears as I walked, but the human pups - toddlers they are called (they must be avoided at all costs if possible) - pulled on them any chance they got.

I personally think that my Beagle bark, which is voiced just as frequently as my Springer Spaniel vocal cords move, does make me very attractive as I seem to get a lot of attention from everyone! My sounds are classified as annoying, alarming, unnerving, distracting, disturbing, and pacifying depending on the observer's point of view.

My birth is a bit of a hazy story; I don't remember much of it. I just remember this burst of light, lots of licking (gee I hope that was my mom!), and then lots of suckling.

AS you may know, Just like other puppies, I was born deaf, blind, and toothless. But there is no need to feel alarmed about all of this, for there was simply not enough room in my biological mom's belly to keep all of us entertained any longer. While my siblings and I waited a few weeks to hear and see the world, we learned to use our noses to find each other and our mom. It was kind of like playing "Pin the Tail on the Donkey", except that there was no Donkey and we didn't have extra tails. Ok, so maybe not quite like "Pin the Tail on the Donkey", but more like a "Push Your Siblings Aside to Get More Milk" type of game.

My early puppy days were all about smells, Mom, food, and my siblings (all six of them). My mom's scent was the first thing that made me feel loved. And the scent of all my siblings gave me comfort and sometimes nausea. Later I found out that my siblings farted a lot which explained the nausea! Next thing I knew, these wonderful things popped out of my gums: razor sharp and really itchy too. So to test them out I nipped, chewed, and bit everything - including my brothers and sisters! Chomping on my siblings was great fun until they returned the favour, I felt like a quilt in the making. This my friends is how I learned that biting too hard hurts! Gradually my eyes developed, and I found out that I was quite a vision! I was the prettiest of all my siblings, and loaded with personality.

Mom's job was to teach us boundaries, self-control, and other puppy manners so we wouldn't hurt each other or ourselves. But I seemed to have altogether missed the lesson on self-control! Oh, the good old days. My siblings and I chewed shoes, curtains, stones, sticks, other dogs' ears, tails, rugs, furniture, doors, stairs, carpet, soap - oh yeah, and I distinctly remember nibbling on human toes and hair. That last one must not have been seen as a charming act as I was trained to stop it as soon as possible. This special training consisted of high-pitched yelping by my new owners, which scared the joy of biting their toes and hair right out of me!

Shortly after birth I was sent to the home of some humans. At first I think I was really sad for losing my dog family, but I guess selling dogs is how some humans make money (which is what they use to buy some things they need and a lot of things they don't!). The short little humans (kids they are called) played with me, carried me around, and tossed the ball for me. They fed me three times a day; I didn't like that at all. I always thought meals should be served every hour around the clock. But I could not reach the pantry door and just had to make do with what was in front of me. Of course I tried stealing a few juicy morsels here and there, but I was always caught and sent back to my kennel, something I never got used to!

To this day I have nightmares about that dreadful enclosure. I think I may have even lost a few teeth trying to battle that metal door which prevented me from exploring the house. I am sure that the metal door had more training as a warrior than me, since it never once opened in response to my rebellious attacks!

As a result of being kept in a kennel, I became claustrophobic. This is a very complicated word humans use for the way I feel when I am in scary little places with metal doors. Even now, as soon as I see a kennel with that metal gate, my brain disobeys me and I panic. I sweat, get dizzy, lose any logic (not sure I ever have much of this anyhow), and then start barking until I spit everywhere. Hard times! Back then, little did I know that these were clear signs of anxiety peppering my already spicy personality!

Despite all my anxiety, my first humans kept me locked up a lot. Worse, they didn't like walking me. So when I was out of the kennel, I would try to amuse myself and keep busy by eating ends of rugs, human pants, socks, furniture, and other such delectable articles. Toilet paper, however, was my favourite: a delicacy if there ever was one! You should definitely try a fresh roll, although any type will do. Otherwise, my days remained rather uneventful until it was time to take me to the vet's office to get "fixed". Up until that point I was unaware that I needed any fixing at all!

The story about the man and his needles is quite unpleasant. This man was called a vet, I guess because it rhymed with pet. This event happened around the time I was about six months old. I liked the smile on the guy's face on our first date. But those needles and thermometers and poking fingers - not to mention the teeth and gum checking business - all made me change my mind after the first five minutes. He even interfered with my claws and ear wax. I mean come on, ear wax?? Then the vet guy decided to give me a needle, which felt like a single, rogue, removable tooth (yes, confusing!!). The needle put me to sleep, which finally was a really pleasant way to spend the afternoon.

When I woke up there was a French-looking hat around my neck, which clearly must have fallen off of my head. I really found that more annoying than the stitches they had given me under my belly somewhere. Anyhow, I never got a really good look at the mess the vet had made down there as the French hat stopped me from investigating my belly. Call me simple, but I would rather look dated than have a plastic hat around my neck and look good!

As a young dashing puppy I chased bees and butterflies whenever I was allowed outside. I learned not to use the rug as a toilet, and even got cuddles on the odd occasions. I believe I was model material. Black shiny fur with white paws and neck, soft gentle brown eyes, and a natural ability to give kisses! I looked like I wore a tuxedo (tuxedo = charming attire worn by humans who wish to look like me). But as I grew bigger, my humans stopped playing with me altogether and no longer had time to take me outside for play and walks. I was locked up in my kennel for very long hours. I must mention that dogs do get bored and depressed. This actually explains why some humans come back home after long hours away to find a chewed up couch next to their un-walked dog!

Sometimes at night I heard really loud growling sounds from the alpha guy and his wife where they slept. Their kids would pretend to be asleep! At such times I was happy to be locked up in the tiny laundry room. The laundry room is where they get rid of their smells so they can hide their identities every day (I wonder how their friends ever find them!).

My life, as handsome and cuddly as I was, had become very boring and depressing. I tried to stay out of my humans' way so I wouldn't get yelled at. I lost the will to chase and play, and even felt like hiding my face just to stay out of trouble. Then one day they just put me in the car and drove me to this place I had never seen before: SPCA (SPCA stands for "Secret Pet Collection Agency"). Apparently my human family no longer considered me cute and didn't want the extra costs of my food and vet bills.

This SPCA was a busy place with lots of barking, sub-standard hygiene, no private quarters, lots of different smells, and high foot traffic. The scents there were really perplexing. I was seriously wondering what kind of outing this was! The upshot was that the humans there were really nice. One human with a big smile on her face came and grabbed my leash, bent over, and cuddled me. She even let me lick her all over, which really made me feel better and helped calm her down too (kissing to anxiety is like icing to a cake). Next thing I knew my humans were gone forever and I was in this large cage with the metal gate, again!!! Even though this was a different gate, it still had the same great training as the one attached to my previous kennel and it refused to let me out!

So after a while I just sat there on the cold floor and pondered my life at seventeen months old. I felt really lonely and wanted to cuddle up to someone or something, but there was nothing around except for a blanket. After some kibbles and a pee walk, they put me back in the kennel and told the metal gate to keep me in. I cried quietly for a while until I was really tired. Then I went to sleep. That first night was just lonely and dark with me and the other unwanted dogs crying, yelling, farting, snoring, or just guarding the new place. But the second night was scary. This explosion called thunder scared me so bad and really hurt my ears too. I shook with fear all night and wished I had a Mom.

The third night the thunder thing was back again to test my hearing, and so we all howled and cried together. The next day some people came to look at us, and they picked this scary looking little white dog (she had fuzzy hair with a French name!) who did nothing but shake and hide. She went home with the nice couple (I wish I had fuzzy hair!). And so all there was left on the fourth day was a bunch of Pit Bulls, a German Shepherd, and me. Those other guys were just as unloved as I was, except for I had the nice ears and they didn't!

On the fifth day, my future mom came walking through the warrior gates!! She seemed very kind and had a very good smell about her too. She stopped and looked at me, then kept walking to the Pit Bull and her new noisy puppies. Right then and there I thought I had lost my chance; who could resist seven cute puppies? Who would pick a black, untrained, depressed, anxious dog over little playful mini Pit Bulls? To top it all off, most humans are pretty big on colour and consider my kind bad luck. Silly me, I thought stepping on somebody else's poop was bad luck! Some even consider black the colour of misfortune (I personally think getting late to an unattended piece of meat unfortunate!). Luckily, my mom walked back to me and mumbled a few words in a comforting, silly voice, which made me feel noticed. I think she is colour blind!

She disappeared only to come back with the SPCA lady to take me out for a walk. I figured at least I'd get a walk and a chance to showcase my credentials while finding out more about this SPCA place I was placed in. It was so romantic: me running ahead of Mom like some undisciplined hooligan, and Mom smiling and using her silly voice on me! I even stopped a few times and licked her face to check for food or extra love. But the walk didn't last too long and I was placed under the metal gate thing`s guard again.

It must have been the kissing, because a few hours later my new mom and her man and a little girl came back to walk me again! Two walks in a day were more than what I had in a month with my other humans. The "Secret Pet Collection Agency" lady told my new family that I was not trained properly and seemed like an anxious, vocal dog who needed a lot of attention. Otherwise, I was described as a really nice puppy who was also crate trained! Hummm, we'll see about that, I thought.

So off we went on another walk. This time my new mom's man walked me and I got lots of cuddles from the little girl. This is when I decided to adopt them and let them take me to their bed where I would sleep for the rest of my life. And so they did. On the car ride to my new home, I sat on my mom's lap to make sure she smelled like me and that she still wanted me. I really liked the little girl too and was hoping she would not decide to compete with me for Mom's attention. I guess I just didn't want her to be sad after Mom picked me over her. But luckily she turned out to be just as crazy about me as Mom! My new alpha didn't get much of an opportunity to make my acquaintance on that day as I just cuddled up to Mom and the little girl!

MY NEW HOME

My detailed profile explicitly indicated how very cute and cuddly I was and included a minor note about me being crate trained, or something to that effect. What they had failed to mention was my sketchy relationship with the metal gate warrior who seemed to have found his way to every single crate, ever positioned at a vantage point. I later discovered the metal gate warrior's training source was *The Art of War* (I should have known!). I walked into my new human's home, ran out to the yard, urinated until I felt dehydrated and dizzy, and then tore around the house in search of the big dog bed. It wasn't hard to find, mind you, although there were a few decoys.

On the first floor there were some long dog beds that the humans themselves sat on and I seemed to be welcome on them too. In the room where the cooking happened some very uncomfortable small dog seats known as chairs were positioned around a wooden guarding post referred to henceforth as a table. So I took a mental note of the location, in case I was in need of a high seat to protect and/or canvas this new kitchen's activities!

The higher floor, which seemed to be strictly designed for exercise after eating chicken in the kitchen, was also accessible to me. No one stopped me, and so I went everywhere. There was one room with a lot of delicious toys and very comfortable warm bedding. But it all smelled like the little girl, who still smelled like a puppy herself, so I decided to be nice and not destroy anything in plain sight! There was another room full of 'buzzing' sounds, which I later discovered was electricity (DO NOT stick your wet tongue around naked buzzing ropes!!). There the alpha sat on a chair and pretended to be busy by pounding on a little box which lay on a different wooden post. Maybe after a few more pounds some bones would be unearthed or something? Whatever alpha was doing seemed to have his rapt attention, like how I feel when I see a dangling bone in front of my face! The alpha's entire ensemble, apparently, is referred to as a desk.

The other room was the one with the big comfy bed. Oh, the sight of that bedding….. So, I just jumped straight on top of it and lay down my head on a fluffy bump (called a pillow). I realized that a pillow was a device designed to help you chew bones in a semi flat position and aid with digestion. I waited to be kicked out, but nothing happened! Low and behold, in came all three humans laughing and saying things in silly voices as they joined me on the big bed.

I got cuddles, kisses, and even had my photo taken. I can only assume that my natural beauty had not been fully realized by them until they saw me in my most favourite position! Baboom, this is what I called a den! Yes sir, I had arrived!

Then, the inevitable occurred.

I was tricked into following my alpha in the small wet room, also known as a bathroom (this is where they take your identity away by washing your beautiful scent off!!). My new mom was standing in the big tub with a smile as she sang to me with her lovely silly voice. Then I was lifted with no dignity and placed in the tub. Admittedly the water massage was nice and so was the oat-smelling foaming thing they put on me. But I was still quite anxious. This I showed by panting, foaming at the mouth, and scratching the bathtub to get out. Then the alpha started feeding me dry sardines (it took me a long time to narrow down the name, and I still fall for that trick) whilst my mom washed my beautiful scent away. Small price to pay! So I decided to trade my integrity for dried, smelly fish treats and learned to live with it. Although I enjoyed the spa like experience, losing the scent of my previous owners made me very sad. Well, I guess change, even a good change, can be uncomfortable!

The first week was a tremendous amount of work with all those smells I had to get used to; two walks a day; homemade meals (that's right!!! New mamma liked gourmet cooking); a king-sized bed; and a few special Ollie-Beds (Ollie = an endearing variation of Oliver). Given my sensitive age, seventeen months old to be precise, Mom decided to take me to doggy training classes. This is a place where the trainer taught a whole bunch of humans how to treat dogs. The lady wasn't too bad, although she was a tease and kept dangling those liver treats in front of my face. In the end, my mom decided that I was perfect just the way I was - until she found out my spontaneous combustion reaction to the doorbell was not a temporary condition!

My description on the adoption paper read: "crate-trained, loving, vocal, and a great family pet". Well, crate was not even an option as I preferred the king-sized bed. Loving; yes that was very accurate indeed. And of course being vocal was what made me noticeable! They called my vocalizations prolonged barking. So it wasn't long before my new humans realized that my reaction to the newcomers (even if they went in and out of the house a hundred times in five minutes) was not a rude bark but a display of my pure joy in receiving them mixed with some everyday dementia! With that great bark, obviously, came the Spaniel's famous shake where my entire lower half would wobble so hard that most people would become hypnotized just by looking at me. So I guess you could say I was a bit excitable. No harm in that; we are all different!

My vocalizations would all start with a trigger like the sound of the doorbell (I sometimes even imagined the doorbell!). Next, a sensation like a thunderstorm would grow in my overactive brain and shoot down my spine. My internal lightning would then tell the rest of my body that it simply had to expend all my energy in just a few minutes. This then came out of me in the form of uncontrollable barking, jumping, and bum shaking. Either of these gestures alone would have been tolerable, but all of them together? Well, they land you in the SPCA!

Thus began my new life on Jordan Street, which was my new hood. Getting to know my new digs proved to be hard work as my new mom and the alpha guy didn't walk me along the same paths. The alpha seemed to be a busy guy, always on the look for new territories, and always in a rush. Peeing was not one of his strengths as far as his person was concerned (mind you, Mom didn't mark either!). Instead the alpha guy liked to tap on a piece of plastic they called a phone (which I have learned not to pee on!), then would wait a few seconds and start talking into the air like anyone was actually listening.

I was especially worried when he would start laughing out loud (you should have seen the looks we got from the other dogs!). I started becoming concerned about this behaviour and thought maybe he should see the vet guy himself. But then again, who was I to point out to my alpha that he was a bit neurotic and tapping wasn't the same as peeing? Although I must admit he was never attacked by other alphas and no one seemed to care about taking my mom or our food away from him despite the lack of urine marking! Maybe this new tapping thing was the way to go? But as crazy as the alpha seemed, he gave me cuddles and pretended he didn't see me when I stole a toy or two to dismantle as a part of my emergency preparedness exercises.

Mom's walks were different. She liked to try different places with me to expand my horizons; after all, who knew what my real potential was? The first time we went for an off-leash hike, I could sense how very tense Mom was. But she took a deep breath (just to see who was around and what the weather was like), kissed me, and took off my leash. Boy O Boy, I loved zig zag walking with no pressure or yanking. All those places I could pee, poo, and dig; and all those people I could bark at! That really was the highlight of my walking career.

My human sister (I shall call her 'Betty' in this book in order to protect her identity) was an immediate source of comfort. Betty greeted me with her beautiful green eyes and a bright smile that revealed a few missing teeth. She let me lick her at will and made sure that half her meals were accidentally dropped from her plate right into my gaping mouth under the table. Betty even let me sit on her lap in the car and never complained about my weight or size. This child was clearly raised in a politically correct home! I knew from the hugs Betty gave me that she deserved to have a loyal brother like me.

Of course it took Mom a lot of leash-on leash-off walks to keep me from barking at some people and some dogs. I guess she just wasn't used to my happy form of greeting. Oh well, I knew it would take me a long time to train her. After all, the woman hid her paw scent by wearing socks and shoes and only peed on higher grounds in secret! This brings me back to a few learning curves we all as a pack had to go through - although I have always maintained my innocence and great intentions!

TRAINING DAY

Sure, I agree; I needed some human manners. I didn't like to share my toys, food, or warm bed, although I liked to help myself to my human's food and bed as it were. Then there was this business with barking/alarming others that didn't go down very well with the humans. And I was frequently troubled by this other thing that vets call anxiety (an emotional disorder only noticed in western dogs!). This condition was really quite simple and not at all my fault. I barked and released saliva when I was anxious (I guess I was trying to calm myself), and I got anxious when I was alone. When I didn't see my family in front of me I felt that they had left me behind and would never come back. So I barked and barked and cried and banged my face on the window to get out so I could find them. Then the neighbours would call Mom and tell her that I had gone 'nuts' and she would come back home to me. No harm done. I just couldn't be left alone.

My trainer, Pam (rhymes nicely with ham), was a tough but lovely human. I especially liked the fact that she smelt like liver all the time. Those liver treats were part of her job! Wow, I wish I were a trainer. She said I had to do the group puppy classes first as my first humans had never trained me. So my mom used a bit of plastic (which seemed to have hidden smells or powers) and registered me for the puppy class over the phone thing, i.e. the tapping device.

I later realized that the plastic bits are called credit cards, which are used as pretend money, exerting power over unclaimed objects (mental note: design one for bone collection activities). The training thing was fine by me as I liked Mom and car rides.

So we went to this place twice a week and trained Mom. In the car, disregarding my fine hearing ability, Mom would crank up the music and sing extremely badly to her favourite songs whilst I suffered in silence. I guess all relationships are based on compromise and my love for Mom made me blind to her lack of singing talent! At the training centre there were about ten humans and their dogs of all different sizes. First we were supposed to sit by our owners' feet whilst the humans listened to the delicious smelling Pam, and then they would practice with us. I was amazed to see a lot of confused looks on the humans' faces. After all, how could they have twenty questions when the teacher had only said ten words?

Be that as it may be, I decided to cooperate. So every time someone dangled a piece of Pam's handout liver, I naturally ran to it to show my eagerness for positive reinforcement learning (big word for giving food to dogs after they do silly things for humans). That did not seem to please Delicious Pam! So she sent Mom and I home to practice our lessons privately and asked us to return prepared the following week. On the car ride home I realized that when Mom was sad or disappointed, she reacted by listening to even louder music while releasing unholy sounds from her throat. Someone just had to tell her not to sing!

So off Mom went the next day and got us some liver treats. She made sure to do some Zen breathing before we started (I do the same thing to prevent myself from eating alpha's breakfasts!). Mom and I were both pleasantly surprised to find out that I'd do almost anything for food! I guess my beagle genes are very strong (which also explains my arthritis and pancreatitis conditions!). I did very well indeed, and Mom upgraded my home training rewards to dry sardines instead of liver. I liked being upgraded! I finished puppy classes on top of my class. Our walks became fun and we understood each other.

My life was running smoothly except for a few minor issues like home alone time and my accursed reaction to doorbells! My reaction to being left behind seemed pretty normal to me. If they gave me a bone, filled up my bowl with fresh water, put the news on, put my cuddly bear toy next to me, and walked out through the door, I would assume abandonment. Abandonment led to anxiety; anxiety made me bark. Simple! However, I too was baffled about the baying sounds that departed my handsome lips as someone entered the house or rang the doorbell. The only other time that a sound surprised me was the farting sounds I produced after a turkey meal on a Thanksgiving night. The smell was just fine and in fact a masterpiece, but the sound really shook my sensitive nature and scared me out of my dreams. So I decided to do daily affirmations telling myself that Mom did it!

On a few occasions I even shocked myself at the sheer strength of my vocal cords. Admirations aside, everyone but Mom felt differently. So, Pam the Ham came back on the scene. She spent hours at our house showing Mom techniques to control my anxious and excitable behaviour set off by the doorbell. She brought more liver treats of precisely the right moisture content and left Mom with more homework. Luckily Mom brought in the sardines again! As Mom and alpha found out later, the biggest culprit in my barking madness at the door was Pappa. Pappa is my Mom`s original alpha who has lost all his hair and walks with arthritis.

Pappa was pretty loud, just like me. For one thing, he loved calling for me as soon as he got out of the car. With Pappa located on the street and me in the house, naturally nothing but sheer pleasurable barking would commence for a few minutes even before anyone realized he had arrived! Then he would ring the doorbell whilst talking to me from behind the closed door, and so I would bark and jump up and down to reciprocate his emotions and welcome him the way he deserved. As soon as he walked in, he would start to sing and dance at the door. As these were both rather abnormal behaviours for most humans, I wondered if maybe he should see Delicious Pam? As he sang and danced for me, I barked and Mom yelled at me and Pappa. Alpha would just shake his head in a very disapproving way and opt for silence; Betty always smiled at me with approval. Pappa ignored alpha; I followed.

Pappa had his own rules. He pretended his English was really bad when he wanted to ignore people and be left alone (I wonder if English is my problem too; Spanish could work for me!). No matter what Mom said, Pappa still maintained the same routine. He walked to the treat cupboard and fed me to oblivion whilst he sang his made up folk songs and talked silly to me. This appealing behaviour also continued at the dinner table where he technically shouldn't have fed me but feigned deafness to my mom's voice and did it anyways! No wonder grandfathers are so well loved (Betty gets away with absolutely anything as long as Pappa has grapes and cookies whilst baby-sitting!). Eventually, Mom produced a list of things Pappa shouldn't do when he came over. But as Mom explained these rules to him, he just looked at me, kept eating grapes (he said they were good for his diabetes!), and nodded his head unconvincingly. I don't think even Delicious Pam could have helped him!

At last Mom gave up on Pappa and called in Pam the Ham again. This time the diagnosis was different. "This behaviour is both normal and uncorrectable in Oliver," said my great dog whisperer. Great conclusion! But Mom wasn't convinced. After hours of watching the very charismatic Cesar Millan and his dog training shows, and subjecting me to humiliating activities like sleeping in my own bed instead of on top of Mom, Mom finally sent Mr. Millan an email. Presumably even the great Mr. Millan thought I was already good enough, as we received no feedback. Like they say, no news is good news. But Mom was still not convinced! So she talked to her invisible friend over the phone, made an appointment, put me in the car, and off we went again to see the vet guy. After violating my person for ten minutes, he diagnosed me with anxiety and an ADD disorder. ADD stands for All Dogs Do (it), so stop fussing and live with it said the vet.

The vet offered Mom some pills to calm my nerves, or was it her nerves? Mom wrapped the pills in mortadella meat cuts before presenting them to me. They made me feel very sleepy, nauseous, and disinterested in life. That made my mom really sad. What kind of a dog would just lie on a couch all day (OK, maybe this is normal behaviour for some bulldogs, but not me!)? After two days, Mom took my pills back to the vet for proper recycling; what an environmentalist! Mom then listened to the vet's advice and just tried to keep my anxiety (as well as Pappa`s) at bay. After that I was just declared a loving, well mannered, handsome, doorbell-reactionary, untrainable fellow. What these episodes taught me was that you have what you have and you can't make lemonade out of beef jerky!

MISUNDERSTANDINGS

I like to think that my humans and I were on good terms. In fact, I was a much loved dog. But it hadn't always been that easy. Much like all relationships, we had to work on all that we had. We accomplished this by using the greatest tool in the *Homo sapiens'* tool box: communication! Maybe those psychologist people who let you sleep in their room and use soft voices to trick you into telling them where you hid the last bone knew something after all (dangerous lot!). First we went through a series of I barked, they barked; I ran, they barked; they ran, I barked; until we all realized that barking was just fun and wasn't accomplishing anything but strengthening our group-barking capacity.

Eventually my mom learned faster than the rest of us that barking (or yelling in human terms) was not getting us anywhere. I too learned how to compromise. I learned to bark for two minutes instead of ten and received a few liver treats for all my troubles. I know it doesn't sound like a fair trade, but I am a really nice guy. However, our misunderstandings did not stop at barking. For instance, there was the time when Mom and alpha had money issues. Mom kept asking alpha who would have come over to our house and stolen money from her purse. Mom's purse was a bottomless bag that housed anything from food and phone to disguising implements commonly referred to as makeup. In addition, I had realized that Mom carried these crinkly things in her purse called bills which I mistakenly thought were there solely to amuse me. So I would help myself to one on the occasion, and as the sound they made under my teeth was so pleasing, I decided to bury them in the folds of my bed. Until such time that I had too many bills and those human laser eyes noticed one sticking out from my bed and they came and took them all back.

I had mixed emotions at first. How rude would you have to be to take what was mine? Then I thought maybe I should have peed on them to mark them as belonging to me. As they carried no scent of mine, maybe they were right to claim them back! Then Mom and alpha started laughing and cuddling me, and then I knew they were just happy to have a handsome son like me who gave them gifts selflessly. However those emotions ran, my mom never left her magic bag on the floor again!

Then of course there was the time when I was trying to figure out what was what and what belonged to whom, and I decided to learn by example. Well, that turned out to be a disaster. I had personally thought that my learning abilities marked me as a much wanted pet. Quick to learn, and even quicker to apply new skills to my settings, I decided to take

matters into my own paws. So every night after alpha
would do his last marking in what they called a toilet,
I would go in and mark the base of the same toilet.
After all, I too was a family member.

I thought Mom would be pleased with the extra
protection and boundaries sat by alpha and I, but
instead she went wacko. She would bend down and
sniff the floor and spray things and wipe them. Mom
had regressed to displaying very odd behaviour for a
human being who washed her own scent off every day.
No wonder she was going through midlife crisis; the
poor woman didn't even know who she was! She called
invisible plumbers on the phone (highly dangerous
people who can erase any trace of pee within a few
hours!). They came over for extensive investigations
and left without any success. Mom would then call
them back and yell at them for leaving the toilet leaky
again. She would mop and spray the floor again and
show all sorts of psychologically disturbed behaviour
until the night she caught me marking!

Well, how was I supposed to know she was mistak-
ing my hard work for a leaky toilet? And of course,
off she went doing the unthinkable: she sprayed the
whole powder room with vinegar (have no fear, no
powder was ever found in the room)! Who does that?
I wanted to complain, but I figured Mom was already
confused about her own identity and maybe this

vinegar spraying thing was like a hormone therapy for her. So I decided to mark outside instead.

And then there was also the organic lip balm issue. I discovered that the shiny stuff was of edible nature after I gave Mom a few hundred kisses one day. After that I took it upon myself to indulge in a few lip balm treats (about seven in one week) to help shiny up my lips. *Burt`s Bees* were my favourites (and I never got sick eating any of his products either!). The job was rather easily done: I would source the location, wait for a quiet moment, remove Burt's product, crack the casing, and devour the contents. Alas, this simple exercise was inevitably turned into a much more complex, secretive operation after Mom discovered all the chewed up casings under the rugs and decided to keep her lip balms in bathrooms or jacket pockets!

The sunny side of all these experiments and learning curves was that my alpha and I learned to trust each other (I guess he makes a lot of mistakes too!). Alpha and I had to work really hard to show me that he was the alpha and that it was OK for us to have only one alpha in the family. This was an ongoing saga until one day I walked on broken glass on one of our walks. My paw really hurt and Mom wasn't there to comfort me. So, reluctantly, I sat down and looked at alpha. To my surprise he stopped talking on his tapping device (aka phone), bent over, and removed the broken glass from my paw pad. But that wasn't all! When he saw the blood, he carried me home and washed my paw clean. After that I bestowed the greatest honour on him and barked my alpha Dad.

THE DIAGNOSIS

I think I've already mentioned that I am a rather vocal, dashing type. This however proved to be troublesome for my new family. For one thing, there was a racist bald guy next door. That's right; this guy simply didn't like the dog race! He even called up the animal control unit to pay us a visit and possibly take me away. My mom and dad and Betty were devastated as they loved me so much already (I am sure that if it came to it they would have offered Betty to the control guy instead just to keep me!). This was unfair, as I only barked when someone came to the door. Now, is it my fault that a lot of people came to visit?

To make matters worse, I suffered from slight short term memory loss. So if the same person who had just walked in got near a door, I would think I had to greet him again! On that day when the animal control person knocked on our door, I barked a few times. Mom and I had just returned from an off-leash park, and so my vocal cords were giving me grief from excessive socializing. When the control guy walked in, Mom picked me up in her arms to show the man that I wasn't aggressive, and I accidentally fell asleep. Given that and my flawless attendance at the new puppy classes (I even got a certificate from Delicious Pam which I tried to eat!), the guy left us alone. He did come back a few weeks later because of a noise complaint, but Mom explained that there had been a bear and a few raccoons in our back yard and that I was in fact doing a great job of alerting everyone to these intruders.

I hope Mom hadn't lied. Since my eyesight is not what it used to be, I sometimes have a hard time distinguishing between a bear, a squirrel, or a garbage can! Anyhow, the control guy just patted me and left. After that I went through a downward spiral where I just barked for no good reason at all. But guess what? No matter how much our racist neighbour complained, the animal shelter guy never came back. He simply concluded that I was a nice dog and that Mom was doing a great job of looking after me. And that was my ticket for some happy soprano barking time!

Busco didn't help the situation much. A loose tabby cat lingering around our street, Busco had taken to sitting on the front lawn in front of our window just to torment me. Mom tried to keep the blinds closed, but I could still smell the offending feline on the other side. To make matters worse, Busco started following us on our walks! Who does that? Naturally, given my fragile nerves, I longed to go off and try to catch him. My wish, unfortunately, was granted one day when I was coming back from a walk with Dad and I smelt the treacherous cat hiding in the hedges a mile away. As we walked by, I snuck my head in, grabbed him by the neck, and tossed him across the street.

Dad was mortified!!! He kept saying "poor Busco, poor Busco". What about me? So we watched Busco limp and commando walk back into a bush and Dad decided to take me back home and report to Mom! What did the woman do?? She walked around the neighbourhood asking everyone if they owned Busco so that she could pay for the vet guy's bill. Astonishingly, on the second day Mom found the cat and his owner! Fortunately no serious damage was done to Busco and the owner was only too happy that I had taught him a lesson. That was the report!

After that I became more confused. My self-esteem was low, my anxiety took the better of me, and I thought everyone was looking at me as a cat killer! My depression took over. I would just eat and sleep and pull back every time Mom tried to take me for a walk. Betty's cuddles and my steak dinners were my only solace. Luckily, we moved from that neighbourhood a few months later. A fresh start was most welcome!

My condition of anxiety and depression must have been alarming to my family as Mom took me to visit a new doctor. Dr. Hayman is a human chiropractor who used to visit the vet guy's office as a mobile practitioner (EVERYTHING moves these days!). Mom had met him when my predecessor, Maggie the purebred beagle, had severe back pains and Mom didn't want to overmedicate her. Instead of medicating Maggie, Dr. Hayman would do a ten-minute alignment manoeuvre and charge Mom a lot. Mom didn't care. She always maintained that she spent Dad's money and she was Ok with that! Such a generous soul she is!

Dr. Hayman had started accepting four-legged patients in his own office once a week. So, to calm my nerves, improve my blood circulation, and help my digestive track, Mom decided I had to see Dr. Hayman every other Wednesday (we even took Betty with us for better alignment). Did that help my anxiety, you may ask? Well, of course not. But I became the proud owner of a curvaceous spine which has further improved the strength of my vocal cords!

It is now widely understood that I have severe anxiety. This may explain why Mom and Dad can't leave me alone for more than a few hours before I start gluing my face to the window with my own saliva! I guess I just wasn't born to be left alone. Luckily for me, Mom and Dad work from home and they kindly put me in my aunt's and uncle's homes when they go out for more than a few hours. Their thoughtful behaviour is promptly rewarded by me when they return. As a thank you, I sleep on Mom's chest all night! Thankfully no one tries to change my condition anymore. They just try to adjust to it. As the famous Sigmund Freud says: "If you can't do it, give up!" And so Mom did.

ENTER THE DRAGON

Just as I had finally settled into my well-deserved life, my humans felt charitable again! I thought I had convinced them that I was all they needed for that good karma thing they're constantly talking about (Karma = what happens when you go over to the neighbour's house and you rip all their dog's toys apart and they don't kick you out). But no, my humans didn't seem to have enough to do as it was.

After my mom, dad and Betty had left me with my human relatives for ten long excruciating days and went on a vacation without me, they came back home with this cute, white puppy with tricky blue eyes. Let me be clear here: I was not fooled. After all, I can smell things! At first I just barked a lot, and then the puppy thought I was her mom and started to lick me, and that really got to me. So I decided to be generous and let her stick around. But I must admit, the resulting depression hit me really hard. Everyone who walked into our home only cared about one thing: cuddling and playing with the puppy!

My mom gave me lots of extra cuddles and walks though. I think her and I both knew that I was an irreplaceable part of the family! Nonetheless, my days as I had known them were over.

Here is how it went down. Some guy had found a box of puppies on the side of the highway, which I personally think had fallen from the back of a DHL Truck (DHL stands for "Doggy Ham & Liver"). This guy had picked up the puppies and taken them home, hence saving them from the big bad highway. Word got to my mother that these puppies were all in need of a home and my mom, being a thoughtless softy (she didn't think about my conditions, now did she?) agreed to take one of the puppies. Little did she know that the Good Samaritan would demand cash for the highway puppies as soon as she was ready to take one home! So my mom decided to pay the guy and leave the Good Samaritan's actions with Karma (see previous explanation about the neighbour and toys).

The new puppy was naturally very cute, as all young are. Their cuteness induces those hormone thingies in you, so you take care of them; biology is a troublesome thing! I personally didn't much like those razor sharp teeth she used to chew my delicate neck with, but something in me told me that I must tolerate this behaviour and teach my competition a few things in return. Believe me, the last thing I needed was to be somebody's mother. Anxiety issues, doorbell troubles, troublesome lungs, a happy home, two walks a day, two massages a day, plenty of car rides, chiropractic visits, sleeping on top of Mom at night, AND a great pedigree. Why would I welcome the little baby crocodile? To top it all off, I could see how Betty's green eyes were on the new puppy all the time; Betty even let the new puppy sit on her lap in the car. I became very self-conscious about my size and my age again!

The new pup turned out to be a girl, and the naming ceremony was utterly ridiculous. It took forever. When they had first brought me home from SPCA, my name was Gulliver (please hold your comments!). My mom had looked at my dad and back at me and then said that there was no way she was going to call my entire handsomeness Gulliver. She also didn't want to make me confused by changing my name too much. That's why they went with Oliver - because it rhymed with Gulliver. I was secretly hoping that they would change Betty's name to something that went nicely with Oliver like PawLiver, RawLiver, or MyLiver! Maybe they didn't care as much for Betty as they did for me! In the new puppy's case, the name debate just went on and on. Willow, Millow, Pillow, Luna, Bindi Schmindi…. At some point I just gave up and went to sleep. When I woke up I heard them saying "Lexi, come here". That's when I knew competition was here to stay! I would have picked Lucifer as the puppy's name myself!

Lexi's background was a bit of an unknown. Mom and Dad thought she was Chihuahua and Husky mixed (I am grateful they are not vets!). Then they thought Corgis had something to do with it all (something about the British traditions?). Finally, on her second vaccination appointment the vet guy determined she was definitely half Jack Russell half Australian Shepherd. Her certificate from the vet guy read "Jack Russell Cross". I reckoned she was just Cross, period!

Like I mentioned before, this puppy just loved chewing. After only two weeks of invading my home, she had chewed the stairs, corners of the walls, carpet, rugs, bed sheets, toys, MY toys, my beds, my ears, my neck, my paws, my tail, shoes, even bed posts! She was completely out of control, and someone had to do something. No five-year-old dog should have to go through all of that.

You may think that all puppies are like this, but I will have you know that I went through my puppyhood with utmost grace and glamour. This highway puppy just behaved like the box she was found in. To my credit and astonishment (as well as everybody else's), I began behaving like a perfect mother to Lexi the crocodile pup (she automatically snapped every two minutes, just hoping to grab a hold of something!!). I never once bit Lexi to discipline her - though my mom didn't think my restraint helped. Mom is still waiting for me to bite the vampire puppy! How else could she learn proper behaviour and turn out as well rounded as me - quite figuratively! First she was just hanging from me with her devilish teeth, and then she wanted my food. I would let her have it when she came close, but then my mom put her on a leash to keep her from eating my meals. And the toys - she HAD to have everything I grabbed! This was very spoiled behaviour.

I must admit that Lexi's arrival caused me to go through a severe bout of depression. This is not something that someone as handsome and well put together as myself should admit to, but my anxiety and depression got the better of me. Luckily my mom was much better at paying attention to me than to Dad (Mom should have picked a furry husband, I think). So I got more cuddles, more car rides, more toys, and at least once a day I had a walk just with Mom. That woman is a therapist!

To my surprise, I started to think of Lexi as my puppy after only a few weeks. So if a dog or a person got too close to us on our walks, I barked a lot. I did not like anyone touching my baby, as vicious as she was. But that didn't last too long. As Lexi got older, I noticed that she was always in front of me and was the first to bark at anything. Then I noticed that I was actually letting her do it! My anxiety came back again; naturally. This was confusing. I was older, and she was just a pup!

I heard Mom talking on her magic phone one day and she kept saying "yup, she is more dominant, yup for sure…..". So either Lexi was more dominant, or I was a woman! Unbelievable, no one at five should find out that they are not who they thought they were! I mean Mom didn't know who she was at forty-five and Dad kept telling her to stop looking so deep. So maybe I needed to look wherever Mom was looking? Maybe we would find ourselves together after all! Up went my anxiety levels again. You know the type where you follow your mom every second in case she leaves you or forgets to feed you? And then you randomly jump on her lap to show her how agile and sporty you are? This ended soon with Mom's help as she called in Delicious Pam yet again.

Pam entered our house smelling divinely of liver and salmon as usual. What an attractive woman! She reassured Mom that my jumping up and the barking at the door was all normal for a dog with my 'condition'. However, she thought Lexi needed to start training right away as she was too smart and dominant to be left alone. Smart!!!! She turned out to be hyper stimulated. How did I know, you may ask? For one thing, there were holes all over my neck and ears to prove that buddy had taken the puppy nipping business way too far! Then there was the matter of the bed sheets! She actually enjoyed tearing them apart, and what is worse is that after hypnotising me, she even got me involved in the act (I mean someone had to hold the other end of the sheets, right?).

Granted, she could gaze at the fireplace, meditate, and watch television up to ten minutes at a time while talking to the animals on the screen, but I wouldn't call that smart. If I smell nothing, I assume nothing. And that's just how it should be. We are descendants of wolves, for crying out loud. I highly doubt the wolves managed to evolve and survive by watching reruns of *Full House*! Be that as it may, Lexi continued with her puppy behaviour until one day Mom found her inside the bedding. That's right! She had chewed all through the sheets and the quilt and was happily extracting all the fluff from the inside of the comforter when Mom caught her.

After finding her and taking her out, Mom was busy cleaning up the mess and sewing things up together when she saw Lexi pull the sock drawer open with her mouth, take a sock out and start to chew. I personally wasn't surprised, as I had seen it happen a few times before, but MOM was not happy. I guess she had finally run out of socks! Back to Delicious Pam, I hope!

THE OUTLOOK

Well, that is how it all really happened. Poor Mom! With Dad being so busy, she now has to continue training the devil child! I personally think it's too rich. After all, Lexi is Dad's baby (unlike me, I prefer my human Mother!) and Dad should deal with this serious issue before the order of the house becomes a national emergency. While Mom and Dad try their best, I can see that the little 'sheep herder' is just up to no good. But, to her credit (and a small one at that too), after only a few months Lexi knew how to sit, fetch, shake paw, heel, and a few other commands that I have never mastered. No big deal. What I lack in training, I make up for with my looks and extra special cuddles.

My mom needs to learn not to say things out loud in front of kids and dogs! As Mom continues her nightly reports to Grandma over the phone, Betty, Lexi, and I update our database to keep up with new family events. This is how I managed to find out that Lexi and I will be abandoned for a few weeks in just a short few months as my humans go to Europe to spend Dad's extra money.

What's next in store for us, you may say? Well, the biggest events for this year include a scheduled vet visit to "fix" Lexi (I don't think she'll ever be fixed, but hey, I am not the vet guy!), and a serious abandonment issue coming up during the next family vacation when Lexi and I will be left with our dog walker! Her name is Annett and she thinks I am just wonderful. God bless her cotton socks, the woman actually thinks I am perfect with natural abilities! She has never complained about a single bark, jump, or shake and treats me like I were her own. She even lets Lexi and I sleep on her bed when we go for sleepovers, though I know that nothing will ever replace my human family!

As we train Lexi and keep an eye on the closet where the luggage is housed, I make sure to remain motionless on Mom's chest as she sleeps at nights so that I can do subliminal work on her. The very last thing we need is Mom and Dad coming back from their next summer vacation with another bundle of trouble in a box!